A Note to Parents

Reading books aloud and playing word game[s] can help their children learn to read. The easy-to-read stories [in the] **Hello Reader! With Flash Cards** series are designed to be enjoyed together. Six activity pages and 16 flash cards in each book help reinforce phonics, sight vocabulary, reading comprehension, and facility with language. Here are some ideas to develop your youngster's reading skills:

Reading with Your Child

- Read the story aloud to your child and look at the colorful illustrations together. Talk about the characters, setting, action, and descriptions. Help your child link the story to events in his or her own life.
- Read parts of the story and invite your child to fill in the missing parts. At first, pause to let your child "read" important last words in a line. Gradually, let your child supply more and more words or phrases. Then take turns reading every other line until your child can read the book independently.

Enjoying the Activity Pages

- Treat each activity as a game to be played for fun. Allow plenty of time to play.
- Read the introductory information aloud and make sure your child understands the directions.

Using the Flash Cards

- Read the words aloud with your child. Talk about the letters and sounds and meanings.
- Match the words on the flash cards with the words in the story.
- Help your child find words that begin with the same letter and sound, words that rhyme, and words with the same ending sound.
- Challenge your child to put flash cards together to make sentences from the story and create new sentences.

Above all else, make reading time together a fun time. Show your child that reading is a pleasant and meaningful activity. Be generous with your praise and know that, as your child's first and most important teacher, you are contributing immensely to his or her command of the printed word.

—Tina Thoburn, Ed. D.
Educational Consultant

Library of Congress Cataloging-in-Publication Data
Fehlner, Paul.
        No way! / by Paul Fehlner; illustrated by Laura Rader.
            p.   cm. — (My first hello reader!)
            "With flash cards."
        Summary: After being denied all the things she wants to do by her parents, a little girl finally gets her way when she asks her grandmother for cookies.
        ISBN 0-590-48514-8
        [1. Behavior—Fiction.   2. Parent and child—Fiction.]
        I. Rader, Laura, ill.   II. Title.   III. Series.
PZ7.F332No   1995   94-32422
[E]—dc20   CIP
                                                                                          AC
24 23 22 21 20 19 18 17 16 15 14 13   8 9/9 0/0

Printed in the U.S.A.   24

First Scholastic printing, January 1995

NO WAY!

by Paul Fehlner
Illustrated by Laura Rader

**My First Hello Reader!
With Flash Cards**

SCHOLASTIC INC.

New York   Toronto   London   Auckland   Sydney

"It's time to get up," said Mommy.

"No way," I said.

"Get up," said Mommy.

I got up.

"Eggs for breakfast," said Daddy.

"No way," I said.

"Breakfast," said Daddy.

I ate eggs for breakfast.

"I want to go play," I said.
"No way," said Mommy.

"I want to see Grandma," said Daddy.

to	said
time	I
it's	Mommy
get	no

eggs 	no
got	way
for	I
breakfast	said 

and	see
want	Grandma
go	up
play	front

did	sit
not	**love**
cookies	**okay**
ate	**Daddy**

I did not go play.

"I want to sit up front," I said.
"No way," said Daddy.

"No way," said Mommy.

I did not sit up front.

"I want cookies," I said.

"Okay?" said Grandma.

Mommy and Daddy said okay.

I love Grandma.

Let's Talk...

The child in this story must do what her parents want
her to do.

What are some of the things her parents want her
to do?

How do you think she feels? Why?

Time for O

All of these words have the letter **O** in them:

for   to   love   no

Mommy   cookies

front   go   okay   not

Point to the letter **O** in each of the words.

Can you find a word that starts with **O**?

Can you find three words that end with **O**?

Can you find a word that has two **O**'s in it?

Order These!

The pictures in each row tell a story. But they are all mixed up! What happens first? Next? Next? What happens last?

Some Days

Did you ever have a day when it seemed as if you never got to do what you wanted to do? Tell about it. What did you really want to do? What did you do instead?

Opposites Time

Words that are opposites mean something completely different. Hot and cold are opposites. Big and little are opposites, too.

For each word on the left, point to the word on the right side that means the opposite.

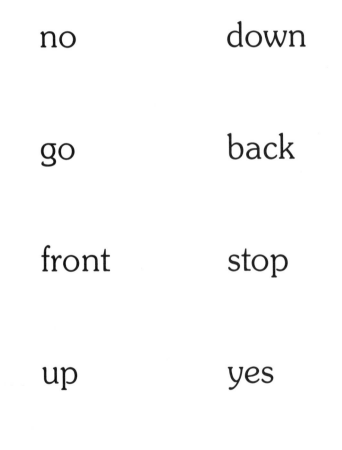

no   down

go   back

front   stop

up   yes

Which One Doesn't Belong?

In each row, one item does not belong with the others.
Point to the item that does not belong.

Answers

(*Let's Talk*) Answers will vary.

(*Time for O*)

    starts with **O**: okay

    ends with **O**: to, go, no

    has 2 **O**'s: cookies

(*Some Days*) Answers will vary.

(*Order These*)

(*Opposites Time*)

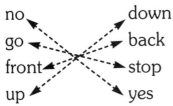

(*Which One Doesn't Belong?*)